A Gift

from

Wild World

Watching
Kangaroos
in Australia

Louise and Richard Spilsbury

Heinemann Library
Chicago, Illinois

Customer Service 888-454-2279

Visit our website at www.heinemannraintree.com

Designed by Ron Kamen and edesign
Illustrations by Martin Sanders
Printed and bound in China by South China Printing Company

10 09 08 07 06
10 9 8 7 6 5 4 3 2 1

Library of Congress Cataloging-in-Publication Data
Spilsbury, Louise.
 Watching kangaroos in Australia / Louise and Richard Spilsbury.
   p. cm. -- (Wild world)
 Includes bibliographical references and index.
 ISBN 1-4034-7225-4 (library binding : hardcover : alk. paper) -- ISBN 1-4034-7238-6 (pbk. : alk. paper)
 1. Kangaroos--Australia--Juvenile literature. I. Spilsbury, Richard, 1963- II. Title. III. Wild world (Chicago, Ill.)
 QL737.M35S64 2006
 599.2'22'0994--dc22
                                    2005017240

Acknowledgments
The author and publishers are grateful to the following for permission to reproduce copyright material: ANT Photolibrary
pp. **20** (Tony Howard), **24** (Dick Whatford); Ardea pp. **5** (Hans & Judy Beste), **11**, **15** (Jean Paul Ferrero), **19**, **21** (Jean
Paul Ferrero); Art Directors & TRIP p. **22** (Australian Picture Library); Corbis pp. **9** (Charles Philip Cangialosi), **14** (Theo
Allofs), **18** (Martin Harvey); FLPA pp. **4** (Norbert Wu), **8** (David Hosking), **12** (Gerard Lacz), **23** (Mitsuaki Iwago), **28**
(Mitsuaki Iwago); Getty Images p. **7**; Lonely Planet Images p. **16** (Lawrie Williams); NHPA pp. **17** (Martin Harvey), **26**
(Dave Watts); PhotoLibrary.com pp. **10** (IFA-Bilderteam Gmbh), **13** (Picture Press), **27** (Index Stock Imagery); Science
Photo Library p. **25** (Art Wolfe). Cover photograph of kangaroos reproduced with permission of FLPA/Norbert Wu.

The publishers would like to thank Michael Bright for his assistance in the preparation of this book. Every effort has been
made to contact copyright holders of any material reproduced in this book. Any omissions will be rectified in subsequent
printings if notice is given to the publishers. The paper used to print this book comes from sustainable resources.

Some words are shown in bold, **like this**. You can find out what they mean by looking in the glossary.

Contents

Meet the Kangaroos

This is Australia, the home of kangaroos.
There are many different kinds of
kangaroo. The red and gray kangaroos
are the biggest and the best known.

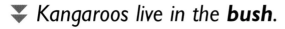

*Kangaroos live in the **bush**.*

Most kangaroos get around by hopping. Some kinds are as small as a rabbit. Other kinds live in trees.

▶▶ Tree kangaroos walk instead of hopping.

Australia's Bush Country

Australia is the smallest **continent** in the world. Most kangaroos live in Australia. Some kinds live in Papua New Guinea and New Zealand.

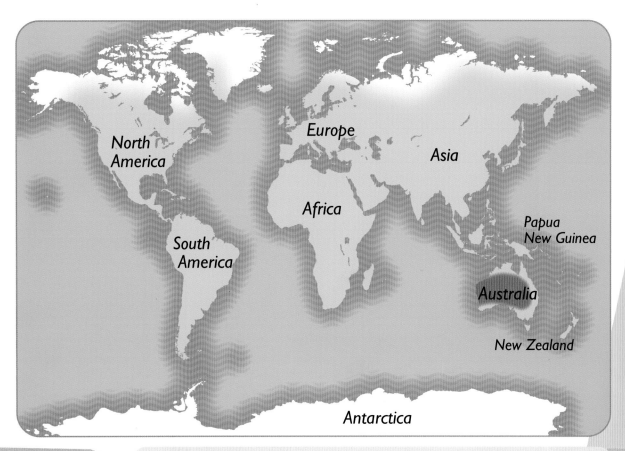

North America

Europe

Asia

Africa

South America

Papua New Guinea

Australia

New Zealand

Antarctica

Key   ● This color shows where red and gray kangaroos live in Australia.

Most kangaroos live in dry parts of
Australia. This land is called **bush**
country. It has many wide-open spaces.

▲ *In bush country, there are grass plants, a few
trees, and some thorny bushes.*

There's a Kangaroo!

This is a red kangaroo. Red kangaroos have short front arms and very big back legs. They have big ears and a huge tail.

ears

short arms

tail

long feet

▲ *A male red kangaroo like this one is big.*
He is taller than most adult humans!

*Young kangaroos are called **joeys**.*

This is a **female** red kangaroo. She is smaller than the **male**. Females have a pouch on their belly. Baby kangaroos grow and stay safe there.

Land of the Kangaroos

In open **bush** country, it is hard to hide. Sometimes kangaroos travel together in groups called mobs. They take turns watching out for danger.

▶▶ *These kangaroos can twist their ears to hear what is going on all around them.*

These kangaroos will stay in the same area of bush land for most of the year.

Kangaroos can travel a long way on their big legs. They usually stay in their **home range**. This is where they live, rest, feed, and have young.

On the Move

Red kangaroos move by hopping on their back legs. Across flat **bush** country, they can bounce along as fast as a car. One hop can be as long as a bus!

▼ *A red kangaroo's big, strong back legs power it up and forward through the air.*

A red kangaroo cannot walk backward. Its big tail gets in the way.

The red kangaroo's huge tail helps it to balance when it hops along. Kangaroos can also walk slowly, using their tail for balance.

Daily Life

It is usually hot in the middle of the day. Many adult kangaroos are asleep. Others are **grooming**. They lick each other's fur to keep it clean.

▶▶ *Grooming is a friendly thing to do.*

The young kangaroos play while the adults sleep. They often tumble around and have boxing matches. Play-fighting helps them grow strong.

◀◀ *When these **male** kangaroos grow up, they may fight for real over **females**.*

Feeding Time

Kangaroos spend a lot of time feeding. They usually feed in the mornings and evenings.

▼ *Red kangaroos rest their short front legs on the ground as they lean forward to eat grass.*

Kangaroos have long, strong teeth for biting.

Kangaroos are **herbivores**. They eat grass and other leafy plants. Their big front teeth cut the plants. Large, flat side teeth chew the food.

Hot and Dry

In summer in Australia, the weather becomes very, very hot. Red kangaroos rest in the shade of trees or bushes.

▲ *Red kangaroos usually sleep when it is too hot to hop around in the sun.*

In **bush** country, there is very little rain. Pools and water holes dry up. Red kangaroos **survive** if they can find grass or other leaves to eat.

▼ *These red kangaroos get the water they need from plants.*

Keeping Cool

Animals that live in hot places such as Australia have ways of keeping cool. Kangaroos lie down on damp mud to cool off.

⬆ *This kangaroo has dug a ditch in the ground to find cool dirt.*

This kangaroo is licking its arms. As the water on its arms dries in the wind, it takes some of the heat away.

▶▶ *Kangaroos lick their arms to keep cool on hot days.*

Baby Kangaroos

This **female** kangaroo is ready to give birth. Kangaroos are **marsupials**. A young marsupial is called a **joey**. When it is born, it is only the size of a small bean.

▶▶ *This pregnant kangaroo will take care of her joey for several years.*

The **joey** climbs up its mother's fur into her pouch. Inside the pouch, it grabs onto a **teat**. It starts to drink its mother's milk.

⏶ *This tiny joey is helpless. It cannot see or hear, but it is safe inside its mother's pouch.*

Growing Up

This **joey** is now four months old. Sometimes he gets out of his mother's pouch to explore. He climbs back in to feed and feel safe.

▶▶ *When joeys first leave their mother's pouch, they are a little wobbly on their feet.*

This joey is about one year old. She stays out of her mother's pouch most of the time. She no longer drinks milk. She eats grass with the adult kangaroos.

▼ *Even big joeys still try to hop back into their mother's pouch when they get tired!*

Dangers

Some kangaroos are killed in fires. Fires spread fast through the dry **bush** in summer. Young kangaroos are also in danger from large eagles and dingos. Dingos are wild dogs found in Australia.

▼ *Dingos follow scent trails to find kangaroos.*

▶▶ *Warning signs tell people where kangaroos cross roads. This protects drivers and kangaroos.*

Many young kangaroos are hit by cars. The young kangaroos that **survive** will grow into adults. They could have **joeys** of their own in a few years.

27

Tracker's Guide

Spotting and identifying the tracks of wild creatures is fun. Kangaroos are usually easy to spot.

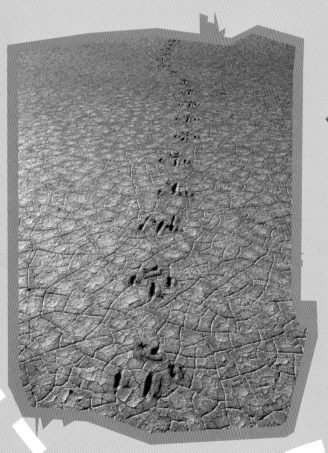

◀◀ *When kangaroos hop along, they leave front and back paw prints as well as a tail print.*

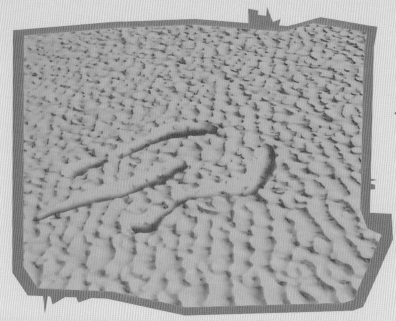

◀◀ A kangaroo also often drags its tail along the ground.

▶▶ You might also find kangaroo droppings.

29

Glossary

bush land that has a few trees, some bushes, and grass plants growing on it. This kind of land covers a lot of Australia.

continent the world is split into seven large areas of land called continents. Each continent is divided into different countries.

female animal that can become a mother when it is grown up. Girls and women are female people.

groom lick or clean fur

herbivore animal that eats plants

home range area of land that an animal or group of animals lives and feeds on

joey baby or young kangaroo

male animal that can become a father when it is grown up. Boys and men are male people.

marsupial kind of animal that carries its baby in a pouch while it grows

survive continue to live

teats part of a mother's body that her young drinks milk from

Find Out More

Books

Eckart, Edana. *Red Kangaroos*. New York: Children's Press, 2003.

Fox, M. *Continents: Australia and Oceania*. Chicago: Heinemann Library, 2002.

Miles, Elizabeth. *Why Do Animals Have Tails?* Chicago: Heinemann Library, 2002.

Niz, Xavier. *Kangaroos*. Mankato, Minn.: Capstone, 2005

Parker, Vic. *We're from Australia*. Chicago: Heinemann Library, 2005.

Pyers, Greg. *Why Am I a Mammal?* Chicago: Raintree, 2005.

Royston, Angela. *Life Cycle of a Kangaroo*. Chicago: Heinemann Library, 1998.

Spilsbury, Louise and Richard. *Life in a Mob: Kangaroos*. Chicago: Heinemann Library, 2004.

Index